It was afternoon when the first snow of the season started to fall.
Chirri and Chirra decided to go for a bicycle ride.

Kaya Doi

Chirri & Chirra
The Snowy Day

Translated from the Japanese by
Yuki Kaneko

ENCHANTED LION BOOKS
NEW YORK

Dring-dring, dring-dring!
The pond in the forest is frozen.

Dring-dring, dring-dring!
They pedal steadily along.
Everything is white,
covered with snow.

Chirri and Chirra discover a door
made of ice and go inside.

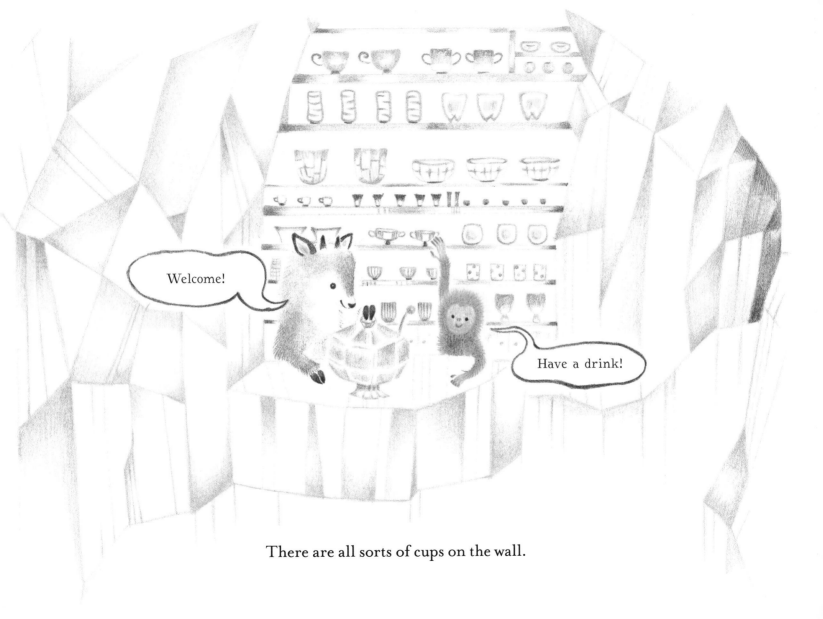

There are all sorts of cups on the wall.

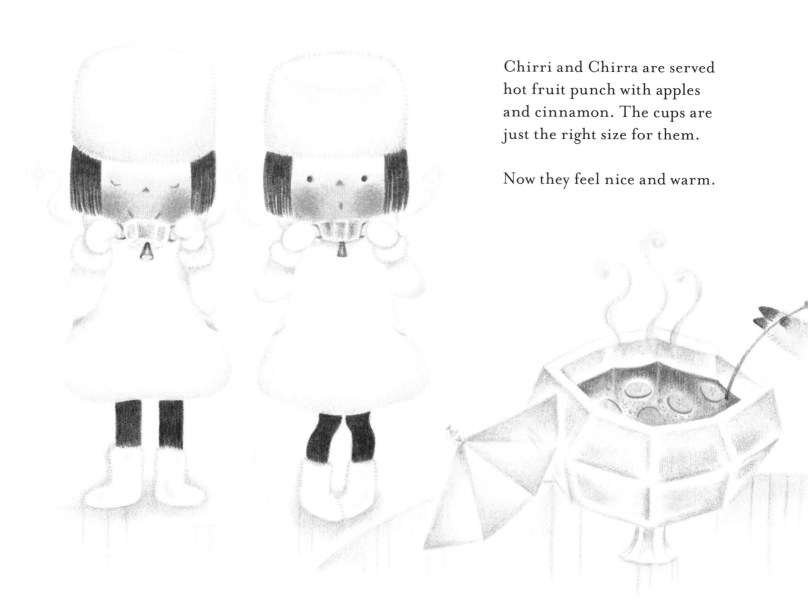

Chirri and Chirra are served hot fruit punch with apples and cinnamon. The cups are just the right size for them.

Now they feel nice and warm.

Dring-dring, dring-dring!
They pedal through an icy passageway.

They come to a great hall.
Everyone is doing all kinds of things.

Chirri and Chirra join a game of marbles.
The marbles are the frozen buds of
many kinds of flowers.

After a while,
  there is an announcement.

Dring-dring, dring-dring!
They follow everyone into a passageway.

It's getting warmer.

A hot spring!
    Chirri and Chirra get in, too.

They dip their marbles into the hot water.
The ice on the buds melts and the flowers bloom.

The water, now scented with flowers,
is just the right temperature.

After their bath,
    something special arrives.

It's rainbow-colored steamed buns from the hot spring, sprinkled with sugar.

Chirri has the orange-flavored one
  and Chirra has the molasses-flavored one.

With their tummies full, they start
  to feel sleepy.

But everyone seems to be going somewhere.
So Chirri and Chirra follow.

Dring-dring, dring-dring!
When they go outside, it has already stopped snowing.

They see all kinds of igloos.

Chirri and Chirra are invited into one
that is just the right size for a bear family.

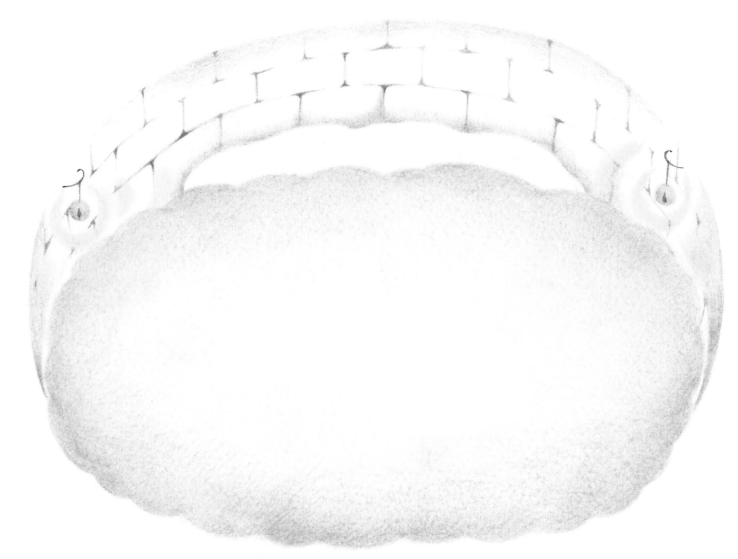

They go inside, where there's a big, cozy bed.

They get under the covers.
And when they turn off the lights…

...the sky is full of shooting stars.

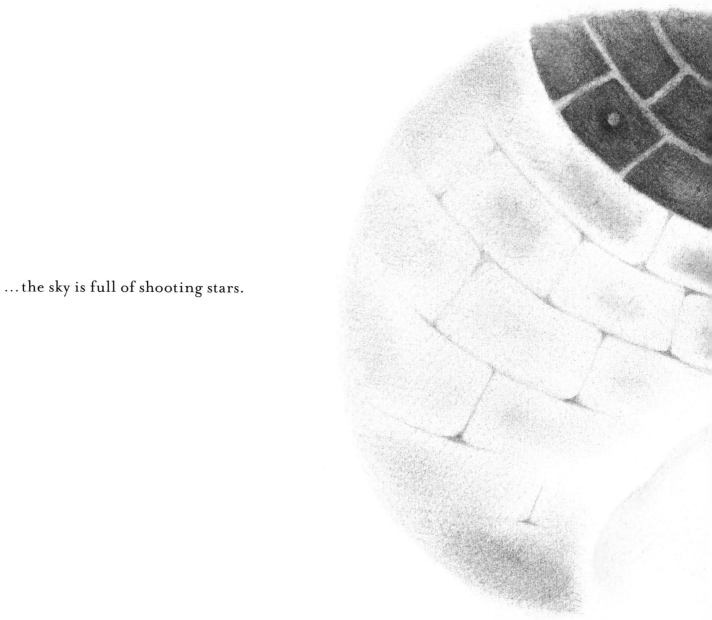

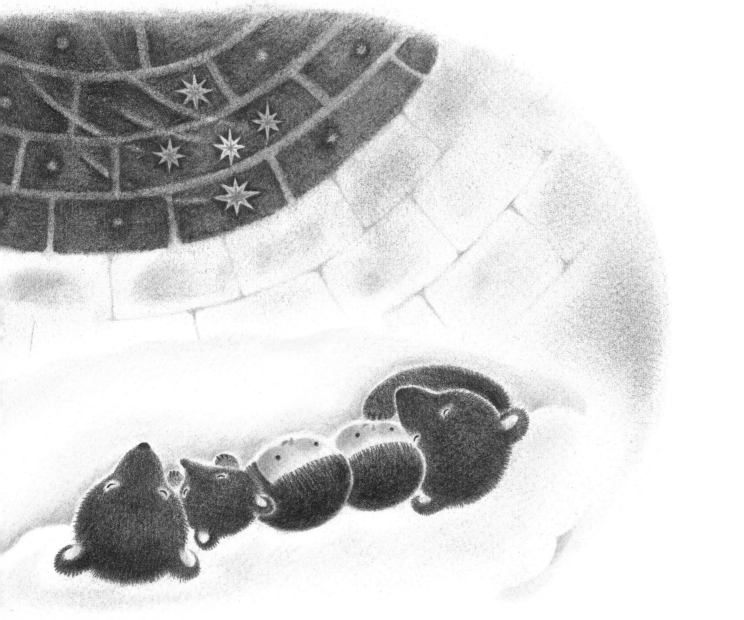

Dring-dring, dring-dring!
Chirri and Chirra have wonderful dreams that night.

Born in Tokyo, Kaya Doi graduated with a degree in design from Tokyo Zokei University.
She got her start in picture books by attending the Atosaki Juku Workshop, a program at a Tokyo bookshop.
Prolific and popular, Doi has created many wonderful books. She now lives in Chiba Prefecture
and maintains a strong interest in environmental and animal welfare issues.

www.enchantedlion.com

First edition, published in 2017 by Enchanted Lion Books,
67 West Street, 317A, Brooklyn, NY 11222
Text and illustrations copyright © 2010 by Kaya Doi
English translation rights arranged with Alicekan Ltd. through Japan UNI Agency, Inc.
All rights reserved under International and Pan-American Copyright Conventions.
A CIP record is on file with the Library of Congress. ISBN 978-1-59270-203-9
Printed in China in April 2017 by RR Donnelley Asia Printing Solutions Ltd.
1 3 5 7 9 10 8 6 4 2